DIVINE
PROVIDENCE

J.B. SISAM

DIVINE
PROVIDENCE

LIVING
LIGHTS
PUBLISHING

SHAKOPEE, MN USA

In Memory of Grandma Sisam

and

To Mom and Dad,
who taught me to always trust in God.

ONE

THE HUSTLE AND BUSTLE of holiday shopping drove people mad with excitement. Lights strung through the little town created an extravagant archway over Main Street. Decorations hugged the frosted green metal of each light pole. Tiny shops were overflowing with lights, decorations and holiday specials.

More Christmas excitement electrified the air, as St. Mark's Catholic Church's Nativity scene lights flickered on. Sally Barnhart held her son's hand as they stared, captivated by the town's benchmark view before them. St. Mark's had outdone itself with the decorations this year.

Twinkling stars shined above in the clear, night sky, and crisp evening air iced Sally's lungs. Frozen breath clouded over her reading glasses. *What store was next on my list?* Glancing down, she rechecked the now worn sheet of paper.

"Com on, hon, we've got one more store before going home."

Christian, the younger of the two Barnhart children, glanced down at a freshly frozen puddle. Sally watched as he delicately placed his weight on the ice. A slight crack shattered the thin icy layer, rushing water over his shoe. "Oops." He said and then giggled.

"Grab my hand." Sally held tight and led him across the street.

As they walked Christian pointed across the street. "Mom, who's that man?"

Sally stopped as his little hand slipped from hers. "Christian, don't let...!" The bags in her hand flew into the air as car tires screeched on the icy road.

The driver leaned out of his window bellowing, "Hey, lady, be careful!"

She stooped to pick up the dropped bags, "Sorry. I just..." Re-grabbing Christian's hand, "Don't ever let go of my hand... okay?"

His lip drooped, "I just wanted to know who that man is." For a six-year old, Christian was consistently curious of his surroundings and the people in them.

"Let's get to the sidewalk." They crossed the street and headed to Cathy's Coffee House at the edge of town. Sally knelt next to Christian. "What man are you talking about?"

"That man." His little finger pointed again.

Sally's eyes fell on the short, stubby man wearing a green coat at the end of the street. His eyes met hers. He took off his grey gentleman's hat, nodded, smiled, turned and disappeared into the crowd. However, something about his blue eyes said, "I'm a friend."

"Let's go say hi to him." She grabbed Christian's hand again while her eye remained on the man. Sally and Christian approached the frozen pond. Laughter rippled through the air as people skated on the town pond, distracting her. She lost the man in the crowd, and her short frame stopped her from seeing over the tall men.

A tap on Sally's shoulder startled her.

"Sorry ma'am, I didn't mean to startle you." The short man's eyes met hers—they were the same height—five feet, six inches. He was older, maybe sixty-five, graying on top with a scruffy white and gray beard. His face was weathered from years of outdoor work. A pair of dainty round spectacles sat on his small button nose. His sparkling eyes and warm smile filled Sally's heart.

"Um..." Sally ran her fingers through her shoulder length blond hair. "I noticed you staring at us. I couldn't help think... perhaps I've seen you around town before. Have we met?" She inquired.

He laughed. "No, I suppose not. But Sally, I have something for you."

How'd he know my name?

He continued smiling and handed her a snow globe he'd taken from his green jacket pocket. "This is for you. There will be a time coming when you'll need this. It will be a comfort for you in sorrow." The small man frowned slightly and began smiling again.

Sorrow? Sally extended her hand to receive his gift. The air electrified as she stared at the beautiful globe. "Thank you, It's... beautiful." The small object fit in the palm of her hand.

The globe's ornate, wood carved base was intricately designed with ice skaters, angels, and stars painted in a bright gold color. Inside the glass orb sat a tiny wooden town that looked like... Providence. Sally sensed something mystical about the globe and shivers rippled the back of her neck. Gently shaking the fragile object, glitter and fake snow circled around and fell across the city scene inside the glass dome.

As Sally stared at the object in her hand, snow fell unannounced. People cheered at the falling snow and she felt compelled to twirl in the fluffy balls flittering about. Her black, wool coat spun out in a perfect circle around her waist. Sally's hair brushed past her frozen cheeks.

The man's laugh bubbled up from his round belly like a freshly shaken soda can, ready to explode. Several people stopped in passing at his laugh. "Sally, this is my gift to you. Remember; in everything place your trust in God. He will be the one to guide you through all things both seen and unseen."

Nick, now stooped down to Christian, "I'll see you later, Christian." He said and ruffled the boy's sandy blond hair with an affectionate hand motion.

Sally was confounded. He knew Christian's name also. "Who are you?" Sally asked.

"Call me Nick." With that he put his gray gentleman's hat back on his head, turned and left.

SNOW CRUNCHED UNDER the Chevy truck's tires as they pulled back into the driveway of the small hobby farm. It was good to be home. The ten mile drive had gone fast, even with bad roads.

"Are Grandpa and Grandma here?" Christian was nearly jumping as his eyes darted back and forth, straining for a sign of them.

She chuckled. "No, honey, but they'll be here soon." Sally turned the engine off. "Go on in and ask your dad to come help me unload."

After Sally opened the door for him, Christian climbed down and raced inside yelling first for his sister: "Rose, Rose... We've got a surprise."

Laughing, Sally grabbed the snow globe from the dash, shook it and watched its glitter fall before slipping it into her coat pocket. "There's the handsome man I married." She called to Zack as he picked up a shovel and began making a path through the snow to the blue pickup.

"Boy, it's sure coming down, isn't it?" He heaved a pile to the side.

"Yeah, tough driving." After Zack set the snow shovel down, she threw a grocery bag into his well-built arms. "Thanks for helping me bring these in."

Zack didn't speak, but smiled as he took the first bag inside. She followed behind, arms loaded with her own bag.

After setting their loads down, she brushed his brown hair away from his eyes. "You okay, Hon? You're usually not this quiet." She stared into his chocolate eyes that melted her heart. "I love you." *I should give him a haircut tonight.*

"I'll be okay, just a lot on my mind. How was your trip into town?"

"Fine, nothing too exciting…. But, there was one thing. I ran into a guy named Nick, and he gave me this." Sally carefully pulled the snow globe out.

Zack took the round object from her hand. He looked it over, and shook it several times. "It's beautifully made. He just handed this to you?"

"Yes, it was kind of weird. Christian noticed him staring at us. Quite friendly."

"Really?" Zack furrowed his eyebrows.

"He was a nice Grandfatherly type." She took the globe from Zack's hand. "It seemed like a nice Holiday gesture of him to give this to me."

Zack laughed. "Did he say why?"

She opened a sack of potatoes and began scrubbing them. "There was something odd. He said this snow globe will bring us comfort in a time of sorrow."

Zack placed his calloused hand on her shoulder and leaned forward to kiss her. "Sally," he said with a squeeze on her arm, "tell me more about it later. You're parents will be here soon." He glanced at the potatoes in the sink. "Let me help you fix dinner."

"You get another kiss for that."

ZACK AND SALLY ACQUIRED the hobby farm from her parents after they moved up-state to help start a new church. The main drawback was once Sally's parents moved north, they only had time to come back for the holidays. The hobby farm is a quiet sanctuary of peace and the aging but comfortable house was the same place Sally and her sister grew up. It wasn't a large home, but its serenity made it perfect.

Sally set a hot pan, filled with peeled potatoes, on the old wood burning stove, which still sits in the kitchen. Growing up, the stove was used to burn corn-cobs and other compost to keep the house warm. Yet, here it sits, cold and in the way. Her hand remained on the pan's handle and the dog sat begging for a magical piece of food to drop into his waiting mouth. "I wonder if Kaitlyn will be able to make it this weekend."

"Hasn't she answered by now?" Zack inquired.

"Apparently there's still a scheduling problem at work." Sally's lip arched upward, "Did I ever tell you, when we were kids, Mom placed a curtain in the stairwell to keep the warm air on the lower level?" She chuckled now recalling it. "I would take my pillow and set it on this old stove, wait for it to get scalding hot, run up the steps and jump under the covers. Then I prayed I would fall asleep before the pillow went cold."

Zack laughed. "Yes, you've told me. Now you have me to keep you warm."

Sally leaned forward and kissed him.

That's how Rose and Christian found them as they rounded the corner into the kitchen a moment later.

"Um…, Mom, Dad." Rose said. She was twelve.

They pulled back from their embrace. "Hi. We were…" Sally said pulling her hair behind her ears.

"I know… kissing." Rose said with a smile. "We finished cleaning our rooms. Can we go outside and play?"

Sally exchanged a quick glance at her husband who nodded in approval. "Yes, you two can go outside."

"Thanks Mom." Rose pulled her stocking cap on. "Come on Christian, let's go play."

Sally grabbed Christian with her arms… "I don't think so…"

"Why?" Christian exclaimed. "I want to play in the snow."

"Where's your hat young man?"

He scratched his chin as a small smile crept across his face. Pointing his finger in the air he said, "Oh, yeah! I was going to get that."

Sally melted, "Okay, but be careful."

"Yes Ma'am." Christian said as he headed outside with his sister.

TWO

SALLY STOOD BACK SATISFIED that she had a table any fancy restaurant would be proud of. She still worked for Jamie's Diner in Providence on occasion. Jamie, her boss, had tried—but failed on several times—to hire her full-time. Sally wanted to be home with the kids and since they were home-schooled, working full-time was out of the question. Each fork had its place. Napkins were neatly arranged on the three plates carefully stacked on each other, and her crystal goblets sat to the right of each dinner plate.

One more candle… there! Sally snatched a match from the box and the sulfur ignited with a strike. It was seven and her parents would arrive shortly.

"Perfect." She said, after lighting all four candles at the center of the table. "Zack, can you call the children in to get cleaned up before Mom and Dad arrive."

Zack walked onto the front porch. "Kids…! Come in and get cleaned up, your grandparents are almost here." He walked back in and turned the oven off. The Prime Rib was done.

It didn't take long before the children bounded up the steps into the house. Rose placed her boots aside while Christian rushed into the kitchen, traipsing mud in with him. Mashing the potatoes Sally called after him, "Ah ah ah ah…! What have I told you about running into the house without taking your boots off?" Sally really didn't need to say more. Her furrowed eyebrow said plenty.

Christian spun around, kicked off his boots and tossed them on the kitchen floor. "Sorry Mom!" and began to run off before Zack called him back to put them away.

George and Marilyn Lykes, Sally's parents, arrived at seven-fifteen. "How's my favorite oldest daughter?" He asked, hardly in the door. He gave both Zack and Sally a hug as he stepped through the door.

"I'm your only oldest daughter Dad." Sally turned to give her mother an equal hug.

"It's good to see you again dear. The roads were terrible tonight. We haven't seen this much snow in years." Her mom glided to the coat closet, took off her hat, scarf and coat, after hanging them up she proceeded with her husband's.

Mom and Dad loved coming back to the farm; to them, it would always be home. Food aromas wafted through the air and tickled everyone's growling stomachs.

Dad cleared his throat. "Everything smells wonderful."

"Thanks Dad! Oh and Mom, I made your favorite garlic mashed potatoes."

Her mother cupped Sally's hand in hers. "That's what I was hoping for."

The greeting was over and everyone sat at the table. Sally glanced quickly around the table. Her heart filled with joy having her Mom and Dad home for the Christmas holiday.

"Dad, will you offer thanks?" Zack asked and Dad gladly prayed.

Sally prepared her famous mashed potatoes, the ones her mother loved. The Prime Rib's juice ran and filled the serving platter and the green beans crammed a nearby bowl. But once their plates were filled, there was no messing around.

"MMM! Honey," Zack's knife sliced through the moist meat; "this is absolutely delicious." He popped a freshly cut piece into his waiting mouth.

"I agree... you certainly outdid yourself with this meal. It's wonderful!" Mom followed suit.

"Thanks." Sally forked potatoes before continuing. "Dad, you and Mom will be staying in Rose's room." She knew Rose didn't like the idea of staying in her brother's room, but if that meant Grandpa and Grandma could come for Christmas, she gladly gave it up.

"I'll help you guys with your bags when we're finished eating."

Zack added.

"I'd appreciate that. This old man can't do as much as he once could." Dad set his napkin down, "Now, what's for dessert?"

ZACK HELPED GEORGE bring their bags in from the car and heaved two suitcases onto Rose's bed.

That should about do it." Zack placed one more bag on the bed.

"Thank you, Zack." Marilyn had already begun to unzip her suitcase to extract her toothbrush from the toiletry bag.

Zack headed out of the room but stopped with hand on door handle. "I'll leave you two to unpack and get settled in. Breakfast will be ready by nine."

"Thanks Zack." George pulled off his shirt as Zack exited the room.

A moment later Zack stood in the kitchen doorway. He watched as his wife placed a dish in the warm water. He loved her. Their wedding day flooded his mind. *For better or for worse.* He didn't realize the true meaning of that, not yet. Little did he know, their lives were about to change.

"Hi." She said.

"Hi." Zack replied. "Would you like help?" It didn't take long before he was holding a towel. He helped Sally finish the dishes.

"Are they settled in?" She asked.

He shook his head, *yes*.

"Good. You know…" She pulled closer to him, so that her body was touching his. "The dishes are done and we're all alone."

"You're right." He smiled and brushed her hair aside.

She whispered soft pleasantries into his ear. He felt her hot breath. "I am, there's only us Zack, only us." And Sally laid her head on his chest.

THREE

THE NEXT MORNING snow on the ground looked like hundreds of sparkling diamonds. The horses ran through the new fluffy substance, spraying it up in the air as if they were tossing tiny crystals. Sagging from the white snow, each tree branch wanted to drop its heavy, frozen contents to the ground.

Standing on the front porch, Sally let the crisp morning air hit her lungs like tiny needles poking at a pin cushion. She glanced at the remaining ice crystals hanging in the air, reflecting the sun's rays. Childhood memories rushed back as the warm sun rays glistened across the front yard. These adventures were fresh in her mind like newly baked bread being pulled out of the oven. Danger, love and excitement—everything important to a kid had no limit to the imagination.

The mug of hazelnut coffee in Sally's hands cooled. Wandering back into the kitchen she began to prepare breakfast for the family. First things first; Sally needed a new cup of coffee.

Hopefully I can have breakfast ready before everyone wakes up!

As Sally poured the pancake batter onto the skillet she hardly noticed soft footsteps behind her.

"Smells really good, honey." Zack wrapped his strong arms around her waist. He leaned forward and placed a tender kiss on her neck.

"Thanks." Zack was being extra affectionate. Maybe this was his way of saying, I'm sorry for the past several weeks of fighting. Fighting had become too common in the household. Zack worked so much and Sally resented him for it, especially the traveling. Bills needed to be paid, and her check at the restaurant didn't help much.

Crackling bacon grease spit as each new piece was added to the frying pan. *Oops.* She recognized that smell.

"Darn, pancakes are burning." Sally usually tried to cook too many items at once. Today was a perfect example; someone would get a burnt pancake… or two.

Zack chuckled. "You fry bacon, and I'll flip the pancakes." Zack grabbed the spatula and flipped the four pancakes one by one. He laughed harder. "I think this one's done." And held up a freshly blackened disc.

"That's not funny!" Sally called over her shoulder.

Zack placed the charcoal pancake in the trash and poured a new one. "Sally, we might need new batter... I had to start over."

Sally placed the last few slices of freshly cooked bacon on the plate and smiled. She pulled the flour out of the cupboard and began mixing a new batch of batter.

"MMMM! That smells good." Mom walked into the kitchen. "Good morning dear!"

"Morning Mom!" Sally spooned the last of the scrambled eggs into a serving dish. The bowl was a wedding gift from her parents. "I have fresh coffee made."

"Wonderful. You're busy—I'll gladly help myself."

"Thanks."

"How'd you guys sleep?" Zack inquired.

Mom sipped the smooth hazelnut brew. "Great, although George snored all night, as usual."

"I didn't either," He said walking into the kitchen. "I smell coffee."

"Hi, Dad." Sally handed her father a cup. "As precious as you all are, I need a little more work space."

"Let me help, Dear. The boys can chat while we set the table." Sally's mom grabbed the plate of bacon and headed out of the kitchen. Glad for her help, Sally grabbed the plates and followed.

"George, looks like you and I were voted off the island." Sally heard Zack say as she left the room.

It wasn't long before the table was set, and Sally called the children. "Rose, Christian, breakfast. Come on down before everything gets cold." She said, then sat down at the table.

Two pajama clad children came bounding down the stairs; both ready for scrumptious food.

"Yummy, pancakes!" Christian said as he climbed upon his chair grabbing a butter knife.

Sally reached over, and plucked the pancake weapon from his hand. "What have I told you about sitting on your knees?"

He folded his legs into proper sitting fashion, and began tapping them against the old wooden chair, ready to gobble the breakfast before his eyes.

"George, would you please say grace?" Zack asked.

"Sure." Dad leaned forward on his elbows. "Lord, we thank you for the blessings you show us each day, and for the family we have sitting around this bountiful table. We pray your blessings on this morning. May your bounty flow into our family this day. Thank you for this meal and for Sally fixing it... Amen!"

"Amen." Everyone chimed in.

The food disappeared.

Although he knew how to use a knife, Sally helped Christian cut his food into manageable pieces. She enjoyed doing special things for him.

Born premature, Christian weighed three pounds, five ounces at birth. The doctors said he might only survive a few short weeks because of an underdeveloped heart. He had Hypoplastic Left Heart Syndrome. The left side of Christian's heart was not pumping enough oxygen to his lungs. Both Zack and Sally had spent many sleepless nights at his bedside, praying he wouldn't die. It had been a long time since Sally prayed to God. When Rose had been born, there were no complications, but with Christian, his uncertain life rested in God's hands. Sally made a deal with God one day while standing at his incubator. If God would spare his life, they would go to church.

They had stopped going after getting married. Several surgeries were preformed to open blood flow in his heart and Christian lived.

Because he lived Zack and Sally decided to honor their petition to God. Zack grew up Catholic so they went to St. Mary's Catholic Church. Both Rose and Christian were baptized in the Church. Sally knew she shouldn't bargain with God, especially when week after week was the same old routine of listening to the Priest. Nothing ever changed.

Ever!

Soon they stopped going altogether.

Zack interrupted her thoughts, "Hon, are we planning on going to church for Christmas Eve Mass?"

"I haven't really thought about it." Sally loved Christmas at St. Mary's. She looked at her Dad. "I'm not sure my parents would enjoy a Catholic service." She was raised Baptist, not Catholic.

"We don't mind where we go," Dad answered. "Zack tells me they put on quite a show at Christmas time." After drinking more coffee he added, "With donkeys and kids dressed up as Mary and Joseph, all the essentials."

"That they do. I've always enjoyed it there at Christmas." Truth to tell, it was the only time we really went to church anymore, although to my parents knowledge, they still went regularly.

"Is their Nativity scene still the benchmark of town?" Mom asked.

"Grandma," Christian piped in, "we saw it yesterday!"

"Did you now? Tell me about it."

"It had baby Jesus and his Mommy and Daddy with lots of angels and they were wearing funny clothes."

"Well, we'll have to go take a look at that, won't we?"

"Yup." His smile split his face from ear to ear.

RUNNING AFTER HIS sister, Christian jumped on Rose, trying to thrust snow down her coat. When he failed he ran into their newly formed snow fortress, planning his next attack.

"You can't get away from me!" Rose scooped up a handful of snow and raced into the fort after Christian.

Sally heard a yelp escape Christian's lips. Rose must have succeeded.

Running out of the fort Christian grabbed another ball throwing it at her. He missed.

Rose taunted him, "Ha ha! You can't hit me!" She reached down scooping snow and threw a snowball at Christian. The cruising snowball connected and Christian face planted in the snow bank.

Sally warned from the kitchen window, "Kids, play nice!"

"Yes, Ma'am." Rose said.

Sally turned to her Mom. "What are you and Dad planning today?"

"We were planning on sticking around here... but we'd like to head into town at some point to finish some Christmas shopping. And it'd be nice to see some friends. Does Jerry Jr. still run his store?"

Sally stopped watching the children through the window. "That sounds like a good idea. And yes he does, his shop looks great!"

"Would you both like to come with?" Dad asked.

Zack's eyes gave Sally the signal he'd like to stay home.

"I think Zack and I need to stay here."

Zack's smile thanked her for catching his memo. "How about the children go with you guys... That is, if you want them. They'd probably love hanging out with you."

"We'd love it!" Mom answered.

As the kids ran to get ready, Sally's eyes fell on the lovely snow globe. It looked beautiful and innocent. Maybe it meant nothing. Nothing had happened yet. The only thing different, as of the last day, Zack was extra affectionate. The unlikely Mr. Nice perception Zack put up had nothing to do with Sally's folks being in town. She was sure of it. Zack's job taxed him greatly. Maybe that's why things were stressed at home. The arguments had subsided, and him being nice now was more like the old Zack.

Zack worked for an auditing company who sent him on several business trips each month. That meant Sally had to fend alone at home with the children while he traveled. They were in agreement that the job required it but it added strain to their relationship.

"Would the children like some good old fashioned ice skating?" Mom asked.

"I'm sure they would love that." Sally smiled, remembering fun times her and her sister had skated on the pond in town. "Don't let them wear you out."

"No chance. This old man may even teach the two kids how it's done." Dad added.

Mom shot him a look. "No you're not. We'll enjoy cocoa while watching them skate on that ice."

Dad poked Mom in the ribs. "Oh, don't take all my fun away." His laugh jiggled his plump belly.

IN MINUTES, Christian and Rose were buckled into the back seat. The two sat on the edge of their seats watching the flying scenery.

"You kids ready for fun?"

"Yes Grandpa." Rose said.

The stunning streets of Providence unfolded before them with decorations hanging from street lamps and garlands crisscrossing overhead, while people milled around St. Mary's nativity scene. A twenty foot high, Douglas Fir Christmas tree filled the town square with ornate gold, purple and red decorations that reflected the late morning sun across the buildings with explosions of color.

After parking they walked down the sidewalk towards Jerry's Pharmacy. George held Christian's hand and Marilyn took Rose's. Joy propelled the children forward. Jerry's Pharmacy was just a block up the road. Marilyn knew the kids would enjoy a quick stop in for a candy stick. She used to take both Sally and Kaitlyn to Jerry's when they were Rose and Christian's age.

"Can we stop at Jerry's" Rose said excitedly.

"Oh, I suppose we can make this exception. And besides, that's what Grandma and Grandpa's are for—to spoil you two." Marilyn said with a smile.

When Marilyn was a kid, her dad would stop in the same store and Jerry's father, Jerry Sr., would give her a piece of candy. Jerry carried on the tradition his father started. Not much had changed in the past seventy years in Providence.

The door jingled as George opened the door for Marilyn and the kids. The store looked the same. The five aisles the store had were filled with over the counter medicine, candy, toys and an assortment of knick-knacks and essential items like soap and toothpaste.

The counter sat near the store entrance. The right side of the counter had the cash register, cigarettes and energy pills, while the left side of the counter had four tall candy jars filled with an assortment of old fashioned candy. The candy Marilyn had in mind for the two grandkids was near the edge of the counter.

"You each can have one… I don't care what Jerry says," Marilyn said, smiling.

"Yes, ma'am." Christian replied respectfully.

"Hey kiddo and kiddoett!" Jerry's hazel eyes sparkled like fireworks as he scooped them up in a bear hug before putting them down again. "I suppose you both want a candy stick?"

He glided back to the counter pulling down the tall glass jar filled with the stripped candy sticks. The jar was filled with different flavors: Red cherry, purple grape, white peppermint and green watermelon were among the most favored. I wouldn't surprise Marilyn if the jars Jerry used were as old as she were.

Marilyn looked over the store some more. Not much had changed. After Jerry's father died, Jerry, Jr. took over his father's Pharmacy. He dedicated himself to run things the way his father did for all those years.

"You each can have one." Jerry's warm voice said followed by a laugh.

"What do you both say?" Marilyn asked.

"Thank you."

"You both are very welcome." Jerry turned to the Lykes', "And how are you both doing? Been awhile."

"We're doing well. And it has been… we'll be here through Christmas."

"Wonderful! How are Zack and Sally? It's been awhile since they've been in here."

"That's Mom." Christian piped up while sucking his grape candy stick.

"Shhh! They're talking." Rose exclaimed while licking her watermelon candy.

"They're doing fine. A little pre-occupied," George answered. "or so it appears. Anyway, we should be going, more shopping to do."

"Well have a Merry Christmas."

And tell that wife of yours the same from George and me. And a Merry Christmas to you also Jerry, it's good to see you again."

"Thanks, Marilyn."

"All right, kids. Let's get busy shopping." Marilyn grabbed their hands and led them out of the store.

SALLY SAT on the living room couch, staring at the snow globe and wondering about the man who'd given it to her. Shaking it several times, Sally watched the falling snow dance around the landscape in the orb. Each snow flake fluttered like an autumn leaf leaving its home on a branch for a new home on the earth's soil. The longer Sally stared, the more it looked like their town. As the glitter settled, she noticed something new inside—something that wasn't there the night before. On the periphery of the tiny town sat a small wooden hobby farm.

Our farm!

"Zack, please come here!"

Zack glided in from the kitchen with a cup of hot coffee warming his hands. "What is it." He asked.

"Take a close look." Sally said handing him the snow globe.

Zack sat down. "It's a nice snow globe." He said, shaking it.

"Zack, take a closer look. Tell me what you see." Sally leaned forward as Zack shook the globe again. He intently watched as the glittery snowflakes floated down around the town inside. "Wow, it almost looks like Providence."

"And...?"

"I don't see anything else."

"Our farm..."

"Our what?" He stared but didn't see what Sally was.

"Our farm, Zack… in the lower corner. House, barn, horses, you name it…. It's all there."

"Isn't that something?" he said finally seeing it. Zack set the globe down next to his coffee. But his voice dropped low as his shoulders sagged, "Sally, I have something to tell you."

Was I ready for this? Something was wrong.

FOUR

GEORGE DECIDED THAT the candy from Jerry gave both the children exponential energy. Exhaustion wrapped its arms tighter around him from his many trips to and from the car. The candy didn't help matters at all. The kids were super energetic to do something, so George rented skates for them to work off energy.

"Whew! I need to sit down." Marilyn expressed as she planted herself in the bench.

"I can't get these…. Argh… on!" Christian exclaimed.

George was already helping him. Rose slipped into hers with relative ease. "There, now you're set."

Christian squealed with joy. "Thanks Grandpa!"

"Come-on Christian... Let's play tag." Rose said, skating circles around him.

George sat next to his wife. "I don't remember it being like this with Sally and Kaitlyn."

"Dear, we were thirty years younger."

"Yeah... suppose you're right." George chuckled while he saw Christian take a tumble on the ice. Before he could say anything, Christian assured he was okay.

The poor kid would learn—at six Christian had more energy then George remembered Sally or Kaitlyn having then. Maybe it was a boy thing...

George considered—if Gideon, his only son, had lived past six years of age, would he have had the same kind of energy? However, Gideon went home to be with the Lord early. That day hovered in his mind like it happened yesterday. The Sheriff and their Pastor showed up at the farm.

"Mr. Lykes?" Sheriff Anderson said, taking off his hat.

George knew something was wrong. "Sheriff, Pastor... What can I do for you?" He asked.

"George..." Sheriff Anderson's voice was quiet. "George, it's Gideon... he was killed by a car as he crossed the street in town." George went numb. "Gide..." The Sheriff caught him by the arm as he began to fall. "Where's Sally... is she...?"

"Sally's fine. She's in the back of the car... she blames herself, but it was an accident."

George walked to the squad car, opened the door and hugged

Sally. Tears formed in his eyes and fell…. Gideon was gone.

He and Marilyn had six wonderful years with their boy. Now, he had Christian—someone he could look after—someone whom he loved so much. God gave George a second chance with Christian. It probably wasn't good to have a favorite grandchild. After all—Christian was the only grandson they had.

When George's arm was stolen by his wife, he entwined his fingers with hers.

"You know what's great about this?" Marilyn asked.

A ripcord pulled at his heart as she rested her cheek against his shoulder. He deeply loved his wife. "What?"

She leaned closer. "We can just sit here and enjoy ourselves while the kids have fun."

He moistened his chapped lips to kiss her on the cheek. "I agree." Marilyn nuzzled herself into his embrace.

EVEN THOUGH he held Sally, Zack's words felt like hammers breaking her heart into little pieces. *How? Why? When?* Pain stole her breath as he confessed his sin… *his affair!* She pushed him away.

How could this happen? Our life wasn't perfect, but it was good. Or so Sally thought. Sure, there had been fights regarding Zack's work, but could that have been the ticking timer of a bomb? Were there warning signs? Had he been out of state too many times away from his family?

"Zack, I don't know what to say… how could you have been so

stupid?" Sally said, as a tear fell. And what did this Rachel have that she didn't?

"Sally, how many times do I have to say I'm sorry?" Zack said.

Silence.

Sally's stomach sank as angry sharks swam within, eating her alive. This was NOT supposed to happen. *We had a decent marriage. I was a good wife... wasn't I?*

"Nothing happened other than the kiss..., I told you, I walked out of the room—I swear!"

More silence. Deafening.

Zack's eyes studied carpet. "I don't know what else to say. I wanted to be honest with..."

"Then don't say anything. There's nothing you can do to fix this...." Sally crossed her arms as tears streamed like rivers down her cheeks. "Zack, we had something beautiful—you've destroyed it!"

His eyes searched hers. "But Sally—"

"Shut-up Zack!" Her vocal cords burned from shouting. She sobbed.

ALL ZACK COULD do was sit. The hurt he saw in Sally's eyes broke his heart. His actions were selfish—simple as that. There was nothing wrong with their marriage. The weight of his confession was like a five hundred pound dumbbell on his chest. Zack wanted to hold his wife—allow his arms to comfort her. She had pushed him away when he tried.

Zack had been on a business trip with another employee. A female employee.

Normally the company sent guys in pairs; however, a last minute change came up—his partner had a family emergency to attend to, so he had to take Rachel along to do an audit on a company out of state. They had become friends through the five years Zack worked for Venture Financial. But something happened the night they had dinner at the hotel.

"Thank you for dinner, Zack." Rachel said.

The way she spoke seemed intoxicating—it was intoxicating. Zack stared into her glowing blue eyes. He was lured in like a fish on a hook.

"My pleasure." Zack said.

After dinner Zack retreated to his room. He took off his jacket and loosened his tie. A glass of red wine and the novel he brought was a perfect end to the day. After reading several chapters, Zack began thinking about Rachel's eyes.

"Zack, get a grip on yourself." He said to his image in the mirror. *I should call Sally.* That would be a good distraction.

As Zack was about to call, three knocks came from his door. He set the phone back on the hook and answered the door. It was Rachel.

"Rachel, what's up?" Zack said.

Rachel cleared her throat. "I was… can I come in?"

He opened the door wider. "Sure, come in… come in." Once she was through, he shut the door. "Have a seat."

Rachel sat on the edge of the bed. "I was going over a couple numbers regarding this account. Something doesn't add up and I don't know where to fix it." She pulled a manila folder out of her bag.

Zack opened the folder and glanced at the pages. "Looks like we'll be here a while... would you like some wine? I have plenty."

Over the next couple of hours Zack helped her find the missing numbers in the audit. After the problem was fixed they kept talking and ordered another bottle. Zack stared into her blue eyes again as a hot wave washed over his body. He swallowed hard. His hands were sticky from perspiration. His tongue was thick and stuck to the roof of his mouth. Rachel was stunning! She glowed like a magazine model—perfect in every detail.

I can't do this. He thought.

She pulled next to him on the bed.

"Rachel, I..."

"Shhh!" Rachel's soft legs wrapped around his waist and she kissed him with hot fiery passion.

A little devil was sitting on his shoulder. *"You can do this... It's okay, Sally will never know. What would it hurt? Rachel is a beautiful woman."*

Zack pulled back from the wet kiss. "I can't! I'm sorry."

"Why, what's wrong? I thought..."

Zack scooted off the bed grabbing his jacket. "Rachel, I'm sorry..." He needed fresh air. "I can't do this to Sally." Zack left his room like a bullet out of a gun.

AS THE CHILDREN happily skated around the pond, George got up to get him and Marilyn hot cocoa from Cathy's Coffee House across the street. While standing in line an electrifying tap on his left shoulder startled him. George turned around.

"Hello, George." Said the pleasant-looking gray-haired man.

"Hi." George noticed the man was wearing a green wool jacket, red scarf and a gray gentlemen's hat. He appeared to be around five feet, six inches tall. Short, compared to George who stood at six-one.

"Lovely day, isn't it?" The man's smile shot warm light into the little café.

"It is. You live around here."

"Oh, here and there. Mostly passing through. Been all over the place." The gray haired man said.

He didn't look like the traveling type. "Business, I take it?" George's curiosity deepened.

"You could say that." The man's chuckle caused people in-line to stare.

It dawned on George that the man had known his name, though he didn't think he'd ever met him before. "What'd you say your name was?"

With a single nod, he answered, "Just call me Nick."

"Would you like some cocoa Nick? It's on me." George asked.

"I appreciate that." Nick said.

"You know, you look like the kind of man who really enjoys chocolate chip cookies and these are the best. I insist on buying you one."

Nick's warm smile split his face as his cheeks blushed red. "You read me right. That's very kind of you."

"You're welcome, one hot cocoa and a chocolate chip cookie coming right up." George placed the order and once outside he handed the strange old man the cookie and steaming cocoa. "Here ya go Nick."

"Thanks again. Tell Marilyn hello for me."

This gray-bearded man knew Marilyn also, "How do you know our names?" George finally managed to ask.

"It's a gift. And I'm sure the lad is sorry for spilling your cocoa."

"What lad?" At that moment George's hand flew to the side as a young boy ran past and knocked his arm. Hot cocoa exploded into the air and landed on the ground. "How did you..." he studied the steaming contents and looked back up at Nick. There was something mystical about Nick... something refreshing. It was visible in the way he was looking at George now.

"Like I said, it's a gift." Nick let a gentle chortle. "George, watch over Sally. She's going to need you today more than ever."

George's face looked confused... perplexed, "Okay, but..."

"Just trust me." Nick said with a comforting touch on George's shoulder. He then quickly turned and disappeared into the crowd eating his cookie.

George hurried to get back to his wife. "What took so long?"

"I had to get two more cups. A young man ran into me." George said, retelling what happened.

She chuckled while keeping her eye on the children.

"But that wasn't the darnest thing. I met a guy named Nick inside. We made conversation and I bought him cocoa."

"That was nice, dear."

"But, that's not the strangest part. He told me my drink would be spilled before it happened. And he knew my name and yours without me giving them."

"Unusual. I don't think I know a Nick, and I've grown up in Providence. Maybe he's visiting relatives and they described you."

George savored more cocoa. "He also told me to watch after Sally, that she's going to need me more than ever."

A commotion from the ice skating pond interrupted George. Everyone was rapidly getting off the ice. He heard Marilyn say, "Get the children."

George got up from the bench hurrying toward the pond. Something was wrong... terribly wrong. A freight train hit his gut—whatever it was churned a metallic flavor in his stomach that made its way to his mouth.

As George neared the rink, a police officer stopped him. "You can't go down there sir."

"Why? My grandkids are there—"

"A large section of thin ice has given way. A small boy skated onto the roped off spot." The officer turned to those still skating, "Everyone off the ice!"

George's heart was pounded by a sledge hammer in his chest. He knew which boy! "Christian."

"Is that your Grandson, sir?"

There was a loud crack. The ice was breaking.

"CHRISTAIN!" George screamed again, running down to the ice.

"Sir, you can't..." the officer pursued.

"Christian, don't move, I'm coming." As he neared the thin ice, George motioned for Christian to slowly inch towards him.

"Grandpa, help!" The tears slid down his cheek, landing on the ice.

George saw the fear in Christian's eyes. "It's okay, Son, come to me very, very slowly."

CRACK! The ice shifted as Christian inched forward.

"Sir, wait... we've got a rope."

Pop, pop, pop... The ice continued rapidly shifting.

George grabbed the rope from the officer. "Christian, I'm going to throw to you. Grab a hold of it and we'll pull you to safety." *Dear God, please help!*

Christian looked terrified.

"You'll do just fine. You're my big boy. Just stand still and wait for Grandpa." George's heart pounded as he inched forward with the rope.

Pop... Pop... CRACK! The ice shifted again under Christian's feet. Tiny air bubbles danced underneath. Christian whimpered as water hit his skates. "Grandpa?!"

CRACK! In that instant the ice gave away. Christian's body briefly hung in midair before plunging under the water.

"CHRISTAIN!" George slid towards the open water as strong

hands grabbed his ankles pulling him away. "LET GO!" He fought the officer, "That's my grandson!"

"Sir, if you want him to live, let us do our job."

George was escorted off the ice. He fought the bulge in his throat. Zack and Sally had trusted him and Marilyn with their children and he failed, not as a grandfather, but as a father. He looked at Marilyn who stood hugging Rose. His shoulders shook with sobs.

"Will he be okay Grandma?" Rose was crying too.

Tears filled Marilyn's eyes. "I pray so dear, I pray so."

George turned and watched as firemen and police began to chuck aside sections of ice and feverishly search to see any sign of the boy.

"How long has he been under?" George heard an officer in diving gear ask.

Two policemen looked at the new recruit, "Three minutes, maybe four."

The diver positioned himself, legs into the water, and dove under. George prayed—it was in God's hands now!

The diver feverishly gazed around the murky water for any sign of a body.

There was none.

His light illuminated two feet in front of him. Even though he had an air tank, it was hard to breathe in water this cold. *Wait, was that?* He strained his eyes.

A body!

FIVE

THE WHOLE WORLD had stopped spinning. The diver had been under for three minutes. *Even if he found Christian, he couldn't have lived.* What would he tell Sally and Zack? Fear gripped his heart, squeezing the life out of him.

"George?" Marilyn said.

"Yes, dear?"

"Do you think?"

"I can't afford to think."

George sat down and cried. He knew Marilyn's heart went out to him. Christian was the only grandson they had, and if he died today.... He couldn't bear losing another boy in the family. Their son was bad enough, but to lose a grandson, it would kill him. George's greatest fear would be his heart giving out—he did not want to leave his wife alone.

George caught a glimpse of water moving. The diver emerged, holding a small body in his grasp.

CHRISTIAN!

The diver pulled the lifeless body onto the ice as paramedics carefully slid over a waiting gurney. They wheeled Christian off the ice, onto a ramp leading to an ambulance. George, Marilyn and Rose followed.

The medic began removing Christian's jacket, hat, boots and clothes from his little form. George noticed Christian's skin had turned a sickening blue, his lips were dark purple and he was not breathing.

Marilyn clutched his arm, "George, what will happen?"

"I... I don't know."

The doors were shutting, "Sir, are you coming?"

George told his wife, "Marilyn you go. I'll take Rose home and get Zack and Sally."

"Sir, we have to go."

"We'll meet you at the hospital."

As soon as Marilyn was in the bus, they left, sirens roaring.

WHEN GEORGE AND ROSE reached the farm, he left the van running so they could all quickly jump in and drive to the hospital. As he climbed the front porch, he didn't know what to say. Words caught in the back of his throat, but he turned the door handle and rushed through.

"Zack, Sally!" He called, hurrying through the empty kitchen.

"We're here Dad. How'd the shopping go?"

The moment he saw Sally's eyes, his heart sank like the Titanic. "Sally..."

"Dad? What's wrong?"

A dam broke in George and the river exploded as he dropped to his knees. "It's... it's... Christian."

Sally grabbed his shoulders. "What about Christian? Where is he? What's wrong?"

"George?" Zack asked.

The broken man looked up, "He fell through the ice in town. We tried to get him..." His sobs slurred his words. "He's on his way to the hospital. Mom's with him."

PARAMEDICS WORKED on the little body in front of Marilyn. She heard the electrical charge of the paddles.

"Clear." Christian's lifeless form jolted upward as the joules of electricity jolted his body.

"Nothing, the EKG's still flat. Give me a hundred."

The humming defibrillator charged in a matter of seconds. "Clear." Again Christian's body jerked upward as electricity impacted against his little heart.

The medic looked worried as he checked again the EKG.

The second medic removed the paddles and began cardio pulmonary resuscitation.

Marilyn prayed silently, *"Lord, please don't take this little one from us. He still has much to live for."*

BEEP!

"Mike, you hear that?"

Mike left his hands on the boy's chest—a faint heartbeart.

BEEP! There it was again… Rhythm.

"Monitor him." Mike grabbed a blanket and covered Christian to warm him.

"Thank you Lord." Marilyn prayed again.

GEORGE, ZACK ROSE and Sally ran through the lobby of the hospital. Mom sat in a waiting chair, her head in her hands. The moment Sally saw her, a bomb exploded in her chest. She knew her baby boy was dead.

"Mom… is Christian…?"

Mom looked up, her face tear stained. "He's in surgery. His heart had stopped for so long it may have suffered damage. Doctor's aren't sure if he can make it."

Sally fell to her knees, every nerve ending in her body—numb. Sally wept.

Zack placed his arms around her. "Sally, the doctor…"

Sally stood. "How's my baby?"

The Doctor stuffed his hands into his coat pockets. "I'm Doctor

Sheets, Christian's doctor. We were able to stabilize your son; however, I need to speak with you folks."

Doctor Sheets led Zack and Sally to his office. His office was small, yet nice. A small oak desk sat in the middle of the room. Several filing cabinets sat to the doctor's left. His degrees and certificates lined the wall behind him.

"Christian's heart has suffered damage." He began. "His heart is not pumping enough blood to his body."

Sally tried to speak—words caught in her throat.

Zack put his hand on her. "Doctor, Christian had an underdeveloped heart when he was born."

Doctor Sheets sat back in his burgundy chair. "I saw the scarring—on his left ventricle. Just from looking at Christian's x-rays, it looks as if Christian was born with *Hypoplastic Left Heart Syndrome*." He asked.

"Yes, he was." Zack took Sally's hand in his and continued. "After several surgeries, his doctor was able to get a larger blood flow to his heart."

Sally recalled those early days of Christian's life. God had pulled him through. She and Zack didn't know if Christian would live, so they prayed. They prayed God wouldn't take their little boy—their Thanksgiving boy. Christian was born Thanksgiving day.

She brushed the tears from her eyes. "Doctor, how is he?"

Doctor Sheets leaned forward, folding his hands. "Again, we were able to stabilize him. I'm going to be very honest with you folks." He paused. Possibly trying to find the right words; words Sally didn't

want to hear. "Because his heart had stopped for too long, his left ventricle is not pumping enough blood to his body… Christian is going to
need a heart transplant."

Heart Transplant? The very thought shook Sally to the core. Her
face, ashen. The Doctor's words were like a bullet piercing her heart—
and the room spun. She glanced at Zack.

Zack, my baby! White hot fire detonated through her skull. Sally
could feel the darkness encroaching upon her as she slammed onto
the floor. She heard Zack's voice… but couldn't make out his words.

And then everything went black.

ZACK WATCHED as Sally fell off her chair—she fainted. "Sally!" He
knelt next to her and picked her up.

The Doctor walked out of the room, to get some water and an
aspirin.

"What happened?" She said, sitting up. Sally squeezed her palms
against her head. "My head is throbbing."

"You fainted." Zack wrote concern across his face. He prayed she
was okay. First, telling Sally of his—affair—now Christian. *Oh, Christian!*

His boy needed a new heart!

He had excellent medical insurance because of his job at Venture
Financial. Zack prayed the health coverage would be enough to pay
for a heart transplant. Six years ago, the average heart transplant was
around six-hundred, thousand dollars. Of course, his health insurance

would pay eighty percent of the coverage—but that still left one-hundred, twenty thousand dollars he needed to cover the surgery.

Doctor Sheet's walked back in, with a glass of water and a cup of aspirin. "Take these; it should help your head."

Sally took the cup of water and aspirin. "Thank you."

"Zack," Sheets said, sitting back down. "I had a chance to look over your medical coverage—and it looks as if they will cover eighty percent. Now, I cannot guarantee anything, however, I am willing to place Christian on the heart donor list. But, it's your call."

The pleading look in Sally's eyes said the same thing Zack had in his mind. There was nothing on this earth keeping them from placing Christian on the donor list. They would figure how to pay the remaining balance. One-hundred, twenty thousand was a lot of money. He'd call the banker in the morning.

"Doctor, put our son on the list. I'll call our banker in the morning to get approval for a loan."

"I want to be honest with you. There is no guarantee that he'll have a heart. You may want to spend as much time with Christian as you can, he may not make it through Christmas. I truly am sorry."

Zack placed his arm around his wife. "Honey, don't worry. We'll get through this."

SALLY'S HEAD STILL throbbed as they walked into Christian's room. The dim room was sterile like the rest of the hospital. Monitors, tubing and wires clenched like vines sucking the life out of Christian as he lay on the bed in an unconscious state. Doctor Sheet's placed Christian on an artificial lung system. His lungs had collapsed because of the water that had filled them.

His skin was pale and his lips, blue. Large dark circles covered his eyes. His hands were wrapped in heavy gauze bandages. Christian looked so small, especially now. *How could this have happened?* Sally thought.

Raw emotion welled up in Sally's heart. Where was God when this happened? Was He on vacation? *How dare God abandon Christian when we asked Him to spare his life at birth? Was this because we didn't go to Mass any longer?* If this was punishment for not going to church, why take it out on a helpless boy?

Sally turned to Zack. "Zack, why would God allow this to happen to our boy?" His tender look warmed her heart and began gluing the pieces back together. The same pieces he had shattered hours before. Now that conversation began to fade.

He wrapped his warm arms around her like giant angel wings keeping her safe as they stared at their son. "It'll be okay—we'll get him a new heart." He said.

SIX

THE SMALL HOSPITAL cafeteria was arranged comfortably. Several tables sat around a Victorian style fireplace, where fire burned inside creating a warm atmosphere for those eating an early dinner. There were several pictures on the wall displaying farms, townspeople and hospital staff employee's of the month. Glued to each picture frame was an engraved gold plaque. Simple Christmas decorations looped the area.

George and Marilyn sat and ate a small dinner in silence. They left Zack, Sally and Rose in Christian's room. George offered to bring them food—Zack and Sally declined his recommendation to eat. However, Rose ate a small sandwich which Marilyn bought for her.

They had seen Christian an hour earlier. Being the grandparents, they were allowed into the room after the immediate family.

Looking at where he lay, hooked up to the machines, sank Marilyn's heart to her toes. Why this happened to the world's nicest boy was beyond her understanding. She believed God knows what He's doing—even though it doesn't always make sense.

A favorite passage of scripture fluttered through Marilyn's mind. *"Trust in the Lord with all your heart, lean not unto your own understanding, but in all your ways acknowledge Him and He will direct your path."* *Trusting* was a hard thing to do, especially when you don't know the outcome. All she had was her trust in God—she prayed Zack and Sally would begin to trust in God.

"What are you thinking about, dear?" George asked.

Marilyn sighed, "Just thinking about how we have to remember to trust in Jesus… that He'll pull our little Christian through." A single tear formed and slid down the crevice of her face and splashed onto the table.

George slid over and embraced her. "Everything is going to be okay. I've called Pastor Bruce to come and pray over Christian. He may never get a new heart but…, at least we can pray for God to do a miracle. We can pray that God will provide a heart for him." George said.

Marilyn sniffed a smile. "That's a good idea. I love you."

"I love you too. Hey…" He said with a squeeze on her arm. "Let's go relieve Zack and Sally, they need to eat."

"George, we already tried that—they declined our offer." She didn't blame them. She would have done the same.

"Well, let's try anyway… what do you say?" He smiled.

"Oh George…!" She laughed. "That's why I love you." Marilyn leaned forward and kissed his lips. "Okay, let's go."

THE CONTINUAL BEEPING of the heart monitor, the breathing machine moving up and down, and other electronic machines wore each nerve ending raw after hours of listening. They sat for most of the afternoon, not saying much of anything. Sally didn't want to say anything—even now to Zack. She was still bitter toward him. She watched the nursing staff move in and out of the room as they checked on Christian. Their world had not begun to spin on its axis yet. Sally figured it wouldn't for some time.

She didn't know what to think any longer. Zack had cheated. Christian lay in a hospital bed and needs a new heart. Order—that's what the world is supposed to have—ceased to exist. And with only two days left till Christmas, would Christian survive? If God was trying to get Sally's attention, this was only going to push her further away. She couldn't figure out why God allowed such things to happen.

Anger gnawed at her mind, while apprehension of the unknown wreaked havoc to her heart. Sure, they went to church, but what good did that faith now have?

Nothing!

Not even our Priest has stopped by to see how we're doing. Sally thought. *Shame on him!* He's supposed to be a minister of God and he didn't even take a moment to care. And Sally didn't care if it was almost Christmas—God didn't care either.

Sally glanced over at Rose, who slept in the bed across from her brother. She looked peaceful as a lamb. She could imagine what was going through Rose's mind. It had to be hard on her. Rose's brother was in a coma and fighting for his life. *How does a kid deal with that kind of stuff?* Sally knew she couldn't deal with it after her own brother's death, all those years ago.

Sally and Gideon had gone into town to get some candy from Jerry Sr. Gideon, her six-year old brother, was so excited he gave her a hug. Sally pushed him away. She hated hugs in public as a kid. There were only two flavors left—peppermint and raspberry. She grabbed the raspberry. Gideon wanted it. They fought and Jerry made her give the candy to her brother. That was the....

"Sally... How are you doing?" Dad asked, quietly shuffling into the room.

"Hey, you guys find something to eat?" Sally asked, rubbing sleep from her eyes.

Dad smiled, "Yes, we did. Nice little Café they've got. You both should go down and get something to eat. You're going to need some food in your system if you want to function."

Zack and Sally exchanged looks, "Dad, we're fine."

Sally felt Zack's hand slid into hers. "Let's go, we need to talk anyway."

The look of hurt on Zack's face was enough to split the sky open as she let go of his hand. "Fine, let's go." And she walked out, leaving her husband to follow behind.

It didn't take long before Zack came up behind at the elevators. *Stupid elevator!* She hoped to have been on and gone, by the time he arrived. It was fine to be in Christian's room with him, now no longer there, she didn't want to be within fifty yards of him—let alone two feet. The door dinged and opened. They stepped through, and deafening silence filled the tiny tube.

"Sally," Zack began, "can we put aside our differences? I already said I'm sorry—what more do you want from me?"

The glows on the buttons were keeping Sally company. "To be left alone."

"Sally…" Zack said.

The tears began to fall one by one and she made no apology for it. "Our son is up there fighting for his life. I've lost faith I you. I've lost faith in God. And my whole world is not the same, Zack. I don't know what else to do."

"You can start by pushing the button for the floor you want."

The third voice sent a shock wave like a typhoon hitting land. They turned to see a gray haired and bearded old man standing behind them. *How much did he hear? All of it?*

Sally noticed he was wearing a gentlemen's hat, a green wool jacket and thin, round wire frame glasses. She thought the glasses accentuated the man's round facial features. His cheeks had a cheerful, rosy glow about them. If she wasn't mistaken, he could pull off a good looking Santa Claus. *Wait… he looks like… the old man from town!* Sally thought. *What was his name?* Oh yeah… *Nick!*

"I'm sorry, I didn't see you back there." The raw embarrassment sliced through her mind. Sally pressed the button for the cafeteria and wiped her tear stained eyes. "What floor are you heading to?" she asked.

"Sally…?" Zack said.

She stopped looking at the buttons when there was no reply from the man. She spun around and her jaw dropped to the hospital basement.

The man was gone. Nick had vanished.

By the time they reached the café, there was hardly a table to sit at. They waited in line for their ordered food to arrive. Zack ordered a cheeseburger with fries, and Sally ordered a Cobb salad. She busied herself on what to drink when Zack tapped her on the shoulder.

She spun around, "What?" A little too harsh; he had something important to say—she saw it in his eyes. "I'm sorry."

"Sally, look over at the table… by the window. Isn't that…?" Zack's voice trailed.

"Oh, my… Zack that's… that's the guy from the…"

"Elevator." They both said in unison.

"I agree." Zack said. "I think he wants us to join him."

The elderly man waved from where he sat. He wanted them to join him. His smile split the cloudy atmosphere when they acknowledged him. After paying, they moseyed over to the table where Nick sat. In-fact, he had all the plasticware set out.

Zack and Sally set their food down.

"How did you do that in the elevator?" Zack asked.

A belly laugh escaped the man's petite lips. "Oh, it's a gift I've got. Zack you can call me Nick."

He knew Zack's name also. *How could that be?* Sally thought. "Um… you're the Nick that gave me the snow globe yesterday."

"Hello, Sally." Nick said. His warm voice relaxed Sally's senses. "How's that snow globe working for you?"

"It's beautiful." Sally said.

"Can I see it? I want to show you something." Nick said.

Sally just looked at the old man, "It's at the house. I'm sorry." She wiped another escaping tear with her hand. "It's been a really… tough day… and… Christian…" The lump in her throat swelled.

Nick's laugh shocked them. How uncouth—She was crying and Nick was chuckling.

"You of little faith; take a look in your purse." Nick said.

My purse? Sally exchanged glances with Zack. What could it hurt? She reached down and opened the bag. To Sally's amazement—more like shock—there it was sitting on top of the contents, the snow globe he'd given her the night before. "How did you… know?" She looked dumbfounded. Sally was certain it was left on the coffee table where Zack placed it earlier. She carefully pulled it out and handed the orb to him.

He grabbed it with both hands. Carefully admired it, as an artist examines his work, before shaking it vigorously.

He remained silent.

Sally watched as the snow and glitter swirled around inside and fall to the ground. She was completely mesmerized by it. Magic circled the air. She couldn't explain it. *Who is this Nick?* Zack mentioned in the elevator that Nick looked like Santa. *Maybe,* but he wasn't a huge fat man. Wasn't Santa supposed to be a lot fatter—or at least well rounded?

"Now Sally, take a look." Nick said.

She smiled at Zack, who looked confused, as confused as she felt. She extracted the globe from Nick's weathered hand. Inside the globe the little pond had several people skating around. They were dancing! There was laughter! It all came from inside the tiny orb. That's impossible…

SALLY FOUND HERSELF standing on the street corner next to Cathy's Coffee House. This couldn't be real. *How'd I get here?* Her thoughts shifted to this and that, it couldn't be real—she was hallucinating.

Perhaps, she fainted again, and this was a dream. *I'm still in the cafeteria.* A white flake fluttered past her eye. Sally looked up as snow fell from the sky above.

"I told you I wanted to show you something special." Nick said, behind her.

Sally spun at the sound of his voice, "Nick, what… what is this? Am I still at the hospital? How'd I get here?" All these and more questions ran around her mind. *I'm losing my mind.*

That was it. *I'm going insane.*

Nick's warm smile was gentle. "My dear child, you have so much to live for. You cannot give up on your marriage, and especially Christian. He needs you more than ever before. Your husband needs you, Sally. Zack can't do this alone—and you can't allow anger to build up in your heart against him."

Tears streamed down Sally's face. "I can't do this. I'm losing my son. I've lost Zack..."

Nick placed a hand on her arm. "Sally, you haven't lost him. He's trying, and you're not forgiving him. You need to forgive him." Nick said.

"I know... I just..."

"Sally, let's head over to Jerry's Pharmacy, there's something I want to show you."

They slowly walked over to the pharmacy, only a block away. People were walking by, laughing and enjoying themselves. Nick remained quite the entire walk. Sally heard voices inside the store. She turned to Nick, but he was gone.

Where'd he go? Apprehensively, Sally pushed the door open. Door bells rang, as she stepped into the warm store. Nick was laughing with someone behind the counter. She walked around the counter. He wore Jerry's apron. *Where is Jerry?*

"Sally, glad you came over." Nick said.

As she rounded the corner she fell to her knees. Sitting on Nick's lap, as good as new, was Christian.

"Christian, oh my baby, my baby." Sally picked him up and hugged him tight. She kissed his cheek and rubbed his hair. Rivers carved their path down her face.

"Hi, Mommy!" He gleefully exclaimed.

Wiping her tears, "How's this possible?" She said. *I must be dreaming.* She didn't care though—Christian was okay—he was here. That's all that mattered. Sally searched Nick's eyes for an answer, but none came.

"Mommy, you want to see what I drew?" Christian asked.

"Sure baby, what did you draw?" He handed her a folded piece of construction paper filled with images of the farm and Barnhart family. "That's beautiful, Christian." Sally said.

Christian grabbed it back and handed it to Nick. "That one's for Nick. He's my friend." He proceeded with a second picture.

Sally, carefully unfolded it. The colors were in perfect order, just as Christian was taught. Purple, gold, blue and reds filled the page. He had drawn a snow globe. *THE snow globe.* Inside the drawn orb a woman, on her knees, was praying. She stared at the image and looked at Christian. "It's me,"

Sally knew. Not sure how, but Sally knew it was her—praying.

Christian smiled with the same big smile he always had. "Are you praying for me, Mommy? I need a new heart." He said.

She grabbed him up and held him tight. "I know baby, I know. Mommy's praying."

"Sally, it's time to go." Nick said.

No, not yet… I don't want to. Sally looked at Nick with pleading eyes, "Not yet, I can't leave my boy here all alone. He needs me." Sally said.

"It's time."

SEVEN

SALLY AWOKE on the couch back at the farm. *How'd I get here?* She thought, not remembering leaving the hospital.

She wiped morning gunk from still sleepy eyes and walked into the kitchen where her mom was making breakfast. The fresh armoma of brewed coffee filled her nose. *I need some!* Sally meandered to the cupboard where she kept the coffee cups and grabbed one from the top shelf.

The tranquil warm liquid filled the ceramic mug. Sally's mouth watered for the wake-me-up juice.

"Morning, Sally." Mom said, while cooking some eggs.

"Hi." Sally sat at the breakfast table. "How'd I get home? I don't remember leaving the hospital."

"Zack brought you home last night. He said you fell asleep eating your food." Mom chuckled. "I guess that salad did you in?"

Sally's mind was still foggy. "I guess so."

She wondered where the snow globe was. *What happened last night?* Sally was certain it was a dream, a very realistic dream. They ate dinner with Nick. That much she remembered... but she also saw Christian, and he was okay. He asked her something... *What was it?* The thought eluded her. *Wake up Sally!*

"Mom, have you seen my snow globe?" Before Sally allowed her mother to answer, she walked into the living room. *Where was it?* There, on the coffee table... right where Zack left it yesterday, undisturbed.

Wait! If the snow globe was here, where Zack had left it... how did it get into my purse?

Sally picked it up and shook the contents inside. She glided back to the kitchen table. Nothing happened.

Just falling snow and glitter.

Frustrated, she shook it again.

Nothing.

What had happened? The events of last night rushed into Sally's mind. Now alert, she remembered Nick had asked for the globe. She knew Zack left it on the coffee table, yet it was in her purse. "Who is this Nick?"

"Nick who, Dear?"

Sally didn't realize she spoke audibly, until Mom said something.

"Sorry, he's the guy who gave me this snow globe."

"That's beautiful, Sally." Mom said.

Sally looked up at her mother, not knowing what to say. She had to say something about Zack's confession. "Mom..."

How does one spill the beans on such a topic. Zack had cheated—there was nothing but that. Her heart still ached at his words. *"And... then Rachel kissed me..."*

If Rachel was close enough to kiss him—he had already let things slide too far. And offer her wine! Sally knew Zack drank wine while away—as it calmed his nerves at the end of a long day—but offer another woman wine?

"...Zack cheated on me." Sally said. She searched her mother's eyes and saw sadness.

"Honey, I'm so sorry—what happened?" Mom said.

Sally recounted the events. How Zack was out of town. About, Rachel coming to his room for questions about the audit. Zack being lured in by Rachel's eyes. The kiss—oh yes, the kiss. That part hurt the most.

Tears formed in Sally's eyes. "Mom, the hardest part is... Zack said he was sorry, but I don't think I can forgive him." Sally's head fell into her hands and she sobbed.

Mom sat there quite, and then said. "Sally... Zack said he was sorry. He mentioned about the elevator incident last night." She paused. "He's trying to be here for you, and you keep pushing him away."

"Mom—"

"I know, dear. You have every right to... but you both have to be strong for Christian. He needs you both, now more than ever." Mom said.

They were interrupted as Rose softly came into the kitchen. "Mommy, I'm hungry." She said.

Rose was dressed in her favorite pink pajamas, imprinted with Santa Claus in his sleigh. Her hair was messy and eyes still groggy with sleep.

Grandma got up and served a plate of eggs, bacon and toast to Rose. "There you are, honey."

"What do you say to your Grandma?" Sally asked.

"Thanks Mamma!" Rose said.

"You're welcome, dear." She turned back to Sally. "Sally, God's word says that we are to cast our cares upon Him, and He will take care of the rest. I don't know God's plan for Christian. And if he goes home to be with the Lord..."

Mom's words caught as she looked down at her coffee. "But, if God's will is for Christian to live—and let's pray that way—then we have a miracle on our hands, and we should give God glory.

"The question I have is this, Sally. Are you going to praise God and trust God, no matter what happens?"

Sally sat wiping tears. Her mother was right. *She was always right.* Mom, had the knack for saying the right thing at the right time—even if it was something you didn't want to hear. Sally lost count of the many conversations they had over the years. Conversations where Mom would quote the Bible and say what needed to be heard.

Again, before Sally could say anything, the doorbell rang.

"Come on in, the doors open." Mom said, loud enough to be heard on the porch.

Who could possibly be here at this time of morning? Sally looked up as a neatly dressed man walked into the kitchen, closing the screen door behind him. He was well-groomed, short black hair and bright brown eyes. His face, well chiseled and tanned. The man looked to be in his early thirties. He was wearing tan slacks and a dark blue polo, that only accentuated his eyes with flecks of red.

"Hello, Marilyn, it's good to see you again. This must be Sally?" He said, then extending his hand.

Sally accepted his gesture, "You must be Pastor Bruce Surls? It is nice to finally meet you." Sally said, with a quiet smile.

"I came at the request of your parents. I'm here to pray with you folks and with Christian." Pastor Surls said.

"That's really sweet of you." Sally didn't know what to say. Not even their Priest came to pray with Christian. St. Mary's should look for a new Priest. Maybe this Surls character was not so bad. After all, he came all this way, just to pray with Christian.

"I understand he needs a new heart?"

They must have told him everything regarding Christain. Sally hoped they didn't mention the marriage problems. "Yes... the Doctor says..." She fought back a lump in her throat. "The Doctor says he might not make it through tomorrow."

The minister took off his coat and knelt next to her. "I cannot begin to imagine what you're going through, but I know that with God, all things are possible."

"How can you say that?" Sally's voice cracked with emotion. "If you were in my situation, you'd be cursing God, not saying all things were possible."

She was okay with her mother throwing God into the mix—but a minister? It was a stupid thought. That's what ministers do best. Give people faith to believe in. But, Sally didn't know what to believe. Zack, cheated and Christian is dying. How much more can a person take in a few days? Sally had turned her back on God years ago. The year Gideon died. That was one thing she never could forgive herself for. It was her fault he was dead.

Sally and Gideon had gone into town to get candy from Jerry's Pharmacy. She didn't get the flavor she wanted, so she was ticked off. Gideon had thanked her with a big hug and Sally pushed him away, "Don't..." It was the last word she spoke. Gideon crossed the street as car hit him head on. Horror erupted through Sally's heart.

"GIDEON....!"

She ran to her brother, now bloodied on the street. She grabbed him and hugged him. "I'm so sorry... I'm so sorry!"

But, Gideon was dead!

"I understand, you're wavering in your faith..." Pastor Surls said.

That statement broke the dam. "I don't have any faith left, Mr. Surls. God took the only faith I had left, and he's dying in that hospital room." Sally scooted the chair back, "Excuse me, I need to be alone." And with that, she left for her bedroom.

ZACK AND GEORGE were out feeding the animals and doing chores in the brisk Christmas Eve air.

"I can hardly believe this year is almost over." George said with an icy cough. "Man alive, it's cold out here."

Zack tied a blanket on both of the horses. "It is cold. And, no, I can't believe the year's almost finished either." He stopped working, "Dad, what do I do now? Sally keeps pushing me away. I just don't know what to do anymore."

Zack would take that moment back if he could. How does one rectify a wrong of this magnitude?

"Zack, you know what the Bible says?" George said.

"What?"

"It says, *'whoever looks at a woman to lust for her, has already committed adultery with her in his heart.'* Zack, it's not that you were about to cheat on her, just the fact that you entertained the thoughts, even just kissing her, you did what you didn't want to do. In Sally's mind, that is what it is, adultery."

Zack took it in. "What can I do?"

"Be there for her. Show her that she can trust you again. Make her believe in your marriage, that it matters to you... above all, pray."

"I'm trying, Dad." Zack said.

"Good and I'll always be here if you need to talk." George said.

"There's something else." Zack said. "Something strange happened yesterday, and I can't explain it."

"What happened?"

Zack grabbed a pair of leather work gloves and slid his hands into them. "When Sally and I got onto the elevator, unbeknownst to us, there was this guy in the elevator. I swear he wasn't there when we got on."

"How's that strange?" George asked.

"He asked us to press a button—Sally and I had been fighting. When Sally asked which floor he wanted, there was no answer—the man vanished. As we approached the Café he was sitting by the window, waiting for us."

George looked up at Zack. "His name wasn't by chance.... Nick, was it?"

Zack didn't know what to say. "How'd you know?"

"I met him yesterday, just before the..."

"The accident?"

"Yes." George heaved a bail of hay into the loft above. "Funny thing is... okay, maybe not funny... but he said Sally would need me, like she's never needed me before."

Zack stopped in mid-throw. The bail hit the floor and he fell on top of it. *That hurt.*

He picked himself up and dusted his jacket off. "How'd he know?"

"I'm not sure. Maybe he's an angel." George said, grabbing another bail.

"Or just a very intuitive man." Zack hoisted another bail. It sailed through the air and landed on target. "Got it that time, Dad."

Both men laughed.

"I don't know. There was something familiar about the man—but I can't place him—it's like I've met him before. And I don't think the elevator counts as meeting him before the cafeteria incident."

"Cafeteria incident?"

"Nick took the snow globe he'd given Sally. He shook it and handed it to her.... Dad, Sally sat staring at the snow globe for ten minutes—without saying a single word. It was like she was somewhere else."

"And she just fainted into her salad?"

"She not only fainted, but Nick disappeared... as if he never existed."

Curiosity crossed George's face. "What do you mean, Zack?"

"Nick handed her the globe and vanished into thin air." That scared Zack more than anything. This apparition named Nick could come and go as he pleased.

"Dad, you understand the Bible better than I do. Does it say anything about angels looking like humans?"

"There is something my pastor said. I don't recall the verse, but it does say, you entertain angels unaware. Like I said before, maybe this Nick is an angel from God." George's stomach grumbled loudly. "I wonder if Marilyn has breakfast ready?"

"Dunno." One more bail flew through the air. "That should about do it." He took off his gloves and hung the bail hooks on the wall.

Zack stopped his father-in-law by the arm. "And thank you for helping me grasp a better understanding of God. I don't fully understand it all. I just pray He spares our little boy."

"My pleasure, son." The men walked back through the yard to the house.

As they walked into the house, Zack heard Marilyn talking to someone. Taking their coats and boots off they proceeded into the kitchen.

"Pastor, glad you were able to come down." George said as he stepped through the door.

The man embraced George. "It's good to be here."

"Bruce, I would like you to meet my son-in-law, Zack."

When Zack finished hanging up his coat, he extended a greeting hand. "Quite the firm handshake you've got. You must be Reverend Surls?"

"Thank you, but please, call me Bruce."

"Alright... Bruce." Zack said as Marilyn handed him a cup of coffee. He sat down at the table. "It is very kind of you to come and pray with our son."

George mentioned, while they were feeding the horses, that they had invited their pastor to come and pray with Christian.

"It's the least I can do for you, folks. I'm really sorry to hear about Christian." Bruce said.

Zack began eating the eggs and bacon Marilyn set in-front of him. "It's hard, really hard." He eyes misted over. "And honestly... I don't know what to think or feel at the moment."

"Zack, the Bible says that God works all things together for the good of those who love God." Bruce leaned forward and folded his hands. "In other words, keep your trust in God. He will pull Christian through. He will provide a miracle."

"We'll be heading down to the hospital later this morning... once everyone is up and ready to go." Zack said.

"Okay, sounds good."

LATER THAT MORNING they arrived back at the hospital. Sally couldn't wait to get back—Christian needed her. Being Christmas Eve, the roads were clear of most traffic. While everyone was having family time, they were at the hospital, waiting for a miracle.

As they walked down the long hallway, towards Christian's room, Sally noticed Jerry from the Pharmacy walking out.

"Jerry, I'm so glad you're here." Sally said, as tears welled in her eyes upon seeing the man.

A single tear dripped off Jerry's nose. "I've brought him some candy from the store.... a grape one... it's his favorite."

Sally wrapped her arms around him. And Jerry collapsed into her arms and wept.

"I'm so sorry!" The big man pulled back from Sally, "Sorry, Sally, I didn't mean to give you a wet shoulder."

"It's okay." She said.

Everyone was silent while Sally and Jerry talked.

After a moment of silence Jerry said, "He looks so peaceful in there.... And I'm praying for him.... Anyway, I wanted to come by before heading home. I've closed my shop early for the holiday." Jerry put his gloves on. "Merry Christmas."

"Merry Christmas also Jerry. Tell your family hello from us." Sally said.

They all watched as Jerry walked down the hall. Once he had disappeared, Sally looked at her family. "Can I have a moment alone with Christian?"

"Sure..., take all the time you need. We'll be in the waiting room." Mom said.

Rose requested to stay behind. She didn't want to leave her mother all alone. And Sally didn't blame her. Sally watched as Rose climbed on a chair next to her brother.

"Hi, Christian... It's Rose." She placed a small teddy bear under Christian's arm. "I brought Teddy for you. I bet you were missing him."

Sally watched as Rose leaned over to his ear and whispered, "Goodbye!" Then she kissed his forehead.

Sally took Christian's hand as another tear formed and fell. "Hi, Honey.... It's Mom." He looked so small and pale. And she had done more crying the past day than in her entire life.

God are you listening? Do something for my son! "I saw you in my dream last night.... You were so happy." Sally choked back a sob. "And you gave me something... a picture of me praying for you."

Sally's fingers rubbed his little hand as she leaned down kissing it. She held his hand to her cheek. "I love you so much, Honey.... And know that Mommy is praying for you."

"Mommy?" Rose asked.

"What is it, Rose?" Sally answered while wiping her nose on a tissue.

Rose became quiet and walked over to another chair behind the foot of the bed and sat. "I don't want him to hear me." Rose folded her hands into her lap. The sadness encroaching on her face overwhelmed Sally's already rampant emotions.

"Rose?"

She looked at her brother, "Mommy, is Christian going to die?"

Sally's heart skipped a beat. She placed her hands over Rose's. "Honey, we don't know.... we're waiting for a new heart. His heart is broken... and it just needs to be... replaced."

Her eyes became set and determined as she captured her mother's eyes. "Mommy, I have a good heart... right?"

"Of course you do. You don't need a new one." Sally said.

She glanced over at Christian again. "That's not what I mean."

"What do you mean, Rose?"

"Christian can have my heart. I want to give it to him." A tear escaped the corner of her eye and fell onto Sally's hand.

The word's caught the back of Sally's throat. "Honey—the doctors are looking for a new heart for him." She wrapped her arms around her daughter and held her tight.

"It's okay, Mommy. I'm ready to die so he can live. He can have my heart."

Sally's heart blew open with dynamite. "Oh, Honey!" Sally sobbed while she held Rose. "You can keep your heart... God will provide one for Christian."

EIGHT

SALLY AND ROSE were both asleep on a makeshift couch formed out of three chairs. Zack smiled at the sight as he sat by Christian's side. He was holding the teddy bear Rose brought from home. Zack remembered the day he brought the bear home for Christian.

While on a business trip to Minneapolis, Zack had some free time so he made a trip to the Mall of America. During a mindless lap around one of the floors, he found a make your own teddy bear store.

Do it yourself? I can do that. After watching several people make their own stuffed animal, he decided to give it a try and make one for Christian.

"Well son, I'm glad he's still keeping you company." Zack tucked the bear under Christian's arm. He closed his eyes for a moment. *I need some rest.*

Zack jerked awake from a dream and glanced at his watch. He'd been asleep for nearly an hour. Sally and Rose were still asleep.

"I need to get out of here... I wonder if there's a chapel here?"

He walked around the hospital and found his way to the chapel. It was a small room. There were four rows of wooden pews. Each wall had a stained glass window back-lit by a light. At the front of the room was a small holy altar with several candles arranged. A cross was af-fixed to the wall behind the altar. Zack took it all in, then lit a candle and knelt in the dimly lit room.

"God..., I'm not much of a praying man, yet I find myself asking you for help. I've messed up... My marriage is in dire need of help. I'm losing my...." His eyes filled with tears. "...I'm losing my son and I don't know where to turn. My son needs a new heart—"

There was movement behind Zack. He looked up. "Hello?"

"I'm sorry." Reverend Bruce Surls said. "I couldn't help but over hear your prayer." He knelt next to Zack. "I came to do some praying myself.... Mind if I join you?"

"No, it's fine." Zack said. "I just needed to get away. Figured there'd be somewhere I could go and have it not look like a hospi-tal."

"Understandable. Do you know that God is listening to you?"

"I'm hoping so." Zack thought for a moment before continuing. He looked at Bruce in the eyes. "You're a man of the cloth; do you think God would answer my prayers, even after I've not held my family in highest regard?"

"I believe if you ask, God will answer." Bruce pulled out a small pocket Bible and thumbed through the pages. "Zack it says in Mathew's Gospel in the sixth chapter, the seventh verse; *'Ask and it will be given to you; seek and you will find; knock and it will be opened to you. For everyone who asks receives, and he who seeks finds, and to him who knocks it will be opened.*

"Or what man is there among you who, if his son asks for bread, will give him a stone? Or if he asks for a fish, will he give him a serpent? If you then, being evil, know how to give good gifts to your children, how much more will your Father who is in heaven give good things to those who ask Him?'

"Zack, God loves you. He sent His Son Jesus for you. That is what this time of year is all about."

Zack studied the ground. "I don't feel that He loves me. I cheated on Sally. I'm not a good person. Yeah I go to church..." Correction, "Sometimes I go to church; but does that really matter?"

"I can understand your frustration towards God. But, He truly is the only one you can turn to. He is the only one who can pull Christian through. Church doesn't matter, as long as you continue to live your life apart from Him."

"I don't know."

Bruce opened his Bible again. "Here, it says in Matthew the first chapter. *'Now the birth of Jesus Christ was as follows: His mother Mary was betrothed to Joseph, before they came together, she was found with child of the Holy Spirit. Then Joseph her husband, being a just man, and not wanting to make her a public example, was minded to put her away secretly.*

"But while he thought about these things, behold an angel of the Lord appeared to him in a dream saying. 'Joseph, son of David, do not be afraid to take to you Mary your wife, for that which is conceived in her is of the Holy Spirit. And she will bring forth a Son, and you will call His name Jesus, for He will save His people from their sins.'

"This is why He came, Zack. Jesus came so that we can have life and life to the full. All you have to do is trust in Him and ask Him for forgiveness. There is no sin too great for Him. The Bible also says that if we repent and turn from our wicked ways, God will throw our sins as far as the east is from the west. This means, God will not remember what we've done."

Zack's tears ran down his face. The first time he'd really cried in the past two days. He figured God had written him off as a reject—especially how he treated his marriage—how he treated Sally. The continual fights they had. The moment in the hotel. God was tugging at his heart. Zack knew he needed God—needed a miracle in his own life. Though it seemed as if life was crashing in around him—here Reverend Surls was showing what he needed most—Jesus.

"God," Zack began. "I'm sorry for everything I've done. I've not a good man. I've cheated on my wife. I've not been the man I should be. I need your forgiveness. I need your mercy." Zack wiped the tears from his eyes.

NICK WATCHED the scene unfold as he stood in the back of the chapel. This was *the* defining moment in Zack's life. And Nick waited a long time for this moment to happen.

As Zack prayed, Bruce placed his hand on the man's back. "I need you to come into my life. I need you to heal my little boy. Bruce told me to ask and you would give me good things. God, asking you for a heart for my little boy is all I can ask for. Please hear my prayer, because I need you—my family needs you."

George and Marilyn walked into the little chapel. They didn't see Nick.

"Amen." Surls said. "George and Marilyn, come welcome your son into the Kingdom of God."

They hugged Zack.

Zack sniffled. "Wow... I've never felt this clean inside."

"That's God taking your sins away, Zack." Bruce said.

"Yeah, I guess He is." Zack said.

"Good for you kid..., good for you. Welcome to the family." Nick said to himself with a glowing smile. He placed the hat, he'd taken off, back on his head and walked out, leaving the Reverend, Lykes' and Zack alone to savor the joyous moment.

NINE

ZACK SAT ON A COUCH facing a warm fireplace in the Café. He was clean on the inside. His parents were religious people and raised him Catholic. Yet, they didn't explain that a person needed a relationship with Jesus to have a successful life—an eternal life. This was the greatest moment of his life.

After sitting with him, George and Marilyn went back to the farm to begin making the Christmas Eve meal. This left him by the fireplace to think. Zack knew Sally would not be in much of a celebration mood—*but how do you put Christmas on hold?* Everything was so different—changing. Zack decided they'd have Christmas around Christian's bed.

"What are you doing here?"

Zack turned around at the sound of Sally's voice. "Hey, you're awake." Zack motioned for her to sit next to him.

"Okay." Sally said, sliding next to him.

"Is someone with Christian?" Zack asked.

"Rose is sitting with him." She rubbed her eyes. "I need some coffee—and you never answered my question."

"What question?"

Sally smiled. The first time he'd seen her really smile all day. "What are you doing here?"

Zack laughed and repositioned himself on the couch to better talk. "Sorry. I've been doing a lot of thinking this afternoon... about life, Christian... our family. I finally realized what I'd been missing all my life."

"What have you been missing?" Sally asked.

Zack wondered how she'd take the next statement. "God. I've not had God in my life."

Okay, so it was out in the open now. Sally sat silent for several moments. Zack searched her eyes for... anything... any sign that he had made the right decision. Of course, he did make the right one—he knew it in his heart. No one could tell him otherwise. However, would Sally see it that way? Especially everything she'd been through the past couple of days. After his confession. After Christian's accident.

"Zack..., I don't know if I can believe any longer. It was okay when the kids were..."

"Sally, I met God today." Zack took her hands in his. "Not the

God that we were taught... I really met Him. He's real!"

"Reverent Surls got to you didn't he? Zack, I never wanted my folks to move away. But they went and helped him start Neighborhood Bible Church up-state. Which is fine and all... but they changed. They look at life differently now. He changed them."

Zack knew the 'He' was not Jesus... but Reverend Surls. Yet, Jesus did change George and Marilyn. And Zack saw the change when they met Bruce.

"Sally, Bruce was right. I've been missing it. We are to have a relationship with Jesus. We've been just going to church and just going through the motions of being a Christian. I was wrong in what I did to you. I was wrong—I should have never entertained those thoughts about Rachel. Bruce told me that if we just ask God to forgive us and confess that He raised Jesus from the dead... we can be saved."

Zack saw Sally's face flush with anger. "So, it's Bruce now?"

She was trying to low blow him. "He told me to call him Bruce." Zack furrowed his eyebrows in frustration. "Sally, that's not the point. The point is... I found God today."

"Well, I'm glad you found a crutch to lean upon. God hasn't been that gracious to me. I can't use religion as a crutch; not anymore." Sally got up, "I'm sorry, Zack; I just can't."

As he watched his wife leave, Zack prayed. "God, be with her. She's having a hard time. Give her something to believe in. Help her see you, that you love her like you love me. Let her see you."

SALLY FELT BAD by the way she just treated Zack. But leaning on God, when all this had happened? It didn't seem logical to her. Of course, the events with Nick were not necessarily logical either. How does one find faith when everything they've ever known is falling apart? She mentioned to Bruce that her faith is dying with Christian.

God, please give my little boy a heart.

That was the only prayer she prayed. If God was listening... maybe He would grant this one request. Maybe Zack was right. Maybe one needs something to believe in. But what would that be? Sally needed good news. She prayed as they walked into Doctor Davis Sheets' office that good news would be on the table. Their boy would finally get his heart. What a Christmas gift that would be.

Sally noticed one of the certificates on the doctor's wall was for best surgeon and another for a humanitarian work he'd done. Probably for helping provide medical care after hurricane Katrina slammed into the gulf coastline. She didn't know for sure—but the thought sounded good. She was having her own hurricane. She needed this doctor to provide a heart for her boy.

"Thank you for coming—"

"When does our son get a new heart?" Zack said, interrupting the Doctor Sheets.

"Zack, Sally... I really don't know how to say this." The man's hesitation was deafening. "I have not been able to secure a heart for Christian."

Sally grabbed Zack's hand and squeezed tightly. "Why? You promised...." Her face flushed with heat as a tear crept down her cheek.

Empathy filled Doctor Sheets' voice. "The best I can offer both of you, is to place Christian in the hospice unit and hopefully give you folks some time to say goodbye. I truly am sorry... there is nothing I can do."

If she could, Sally would throw the desk at the good doctor. "You promised! My baby needs a heart!" Sally slammed her fist into the oak desk. She thought her hand went through, splintering the wood. "You speak as if he's already dead! I'm not going to sit by and let my son die.... I need a heart for my baby... I need... You have to... he needs..."

Sally wept.

Doctor Sheets took of his spectacles and laid them on the desk. "I'll see what I can do." He bent down and picked up his briefcase, "If you'll excuse me, I will make another phone call—but... honestly, I cannot make any promises. Stay as long as you'd like, just lock my office door when you're done."

"Thank you." Zack said.

"Take care of her, she needs you." Davis said.

"I know."

GEORGE AND MARILYN arrived back at the hospital with the food they'd prepared. Zack called and explained everything the doctor said. George's heart sank at the news. He prayed all day that God would bring about a miracle. Everyone wanted more time. Now, Christian might make it through Christmas, but again, there were no guarantees. Only God knew. Only God could provide a miracle.

"Marilyn?" George asked while they walked down the hospital corridor.

"Yes, dear?"

"I was praying and reading my Bible last night. Jesus reminded me that He's in control, and I'm not. Do you remember what the Good Books says about trusting in God?"

Marilyn smiled. "I do; *'Trust in the Lord with all your heart, lean not on your own understanding, but in all your ways, acknowledge Him and He will direct your paths.'*"

"Right, Proverbs chapter three, verses five and six. I want to know what His plans are, but I don't know."

"We keep trusting... that's what we do." Marilyn said.

They came to the new room Christian had been moved to. The room was quaint and small. The bed where Christian lay was to the right. A small couch and coffee table sat to the left of the door. Zack and Sally were sitting on the two lounge chairs next to the couch.

There was no buzzing lung respirators or machines, just the constant beep from the heart monitor positioned to the right of the bed. This was the final move—the place where they sent people to die.

"How's he doing dear?" George asked.

A small smile crept across Sally's lips. "He's still sleeping. He hasn't woken up." She glanced at the ground. "Mom, they took him off his respirator. They don't expect him to live much past tomorrow.

Why does God let this happen?" She blew her nose on a Kleenex.

George's heart reached out to Sally, wanting to comfort the pain she was feeling.

Marilyn was already holding her. "Honey, Jesus said that He'd never leave us nor forsake us. It's a promise we can hold on to."

Sally pulled back from her mother's embrace. "I know... What did you guys bring for dinner?"

Sally changed the subject, and George noticed it.

"Oh, we brought a salad, potato soup and some buttered bread-sticks." Marilyn said.

THEY TURNED Christian's room into a small, make-shift dining room. It was hard to eat, especially as he lay there—unmoving. Sally hoped to wake from this nightmare. With each passing moment—it was a moment they'd never get back. A moment Sally would never get back. Christmas was fast encroaching. She knew there'd be no celebration. No love, no gifts, no dinner... just mourning. Nothing more, nothing less. Nobody wanted to go, or stay. And Sally's energy drained with each passing moment.

Conversation lulled to the point of no talking. Zack and George had finished their bowls of soup, while Mom and Sally only had a few spoonfuls.

"We can't just sit here and do nothing." Dad said. "I say we start saying the things Christian has blessed us with."

"That's a wonderful idea." Mom said.

Sally couldn't take it any loner. "Would you all just stop!"

"Sally—" Zack was cut off.

"We sit here, pretending like nothing's happening; eating a meal, trying to celebrate Christmas... don't you get it...? There's not going to be Christmas this year!"

Mom started talking. "Sally... we're not pretending. We are trying—"

"Just stop!" Sally yelled, got up and left the room.

TEN

SALLY STEPPED THROUGH the front door of the hospital. Surprisingly enough, the tears hadn't frozen to her face. She let the ice-cold air fill her lungs. She watched people come and go, each talking happily. *How can they be so happy?*

"Because of the Reason for the Season."

Sally spun around at the familiar voice. "Nick?"

"Hello, Sally." Nick said, warmly.

Sally stuffed her hands into her coat pockets. "What are you doing here?"

"Answering your question." He said emphatically.

"What? What question?" Sally asked, as curiosity wrapped its large arms around her mind.

"You were wondering why all these people could be so happy. And my response was... *'Because of the Reason for the Season.'*" Nick lightly chuckled.

Sally just stared at him.

"Sally, God wants us to count it all joy when we encounter various trials. Trust me, I know. This is a test you must face." Nick wrapped his scarf tighter. "You have been asking yourself the question; *'Why does God allow this to happen'* When the proper question is, What is it God wants to show me?"

"How can I ask that, when Christian is lying up there dying?"

"God doesn't answer the why questions of life, Sally. And He will never allow us to go through something that He knows we can't handle. Sally... this is your Christmas story."

Rivers rushed down her cheeks. "How can I celebrate Christmas... when everything is not so merry? My son is dying—and there's nothing I can do to stop it." Sally tried wiping the tears, yet they came faster than she could wipe. "I love my son so much—I can't let him go—he has to live!"

"Do you have the snow globe I gave you?" Nick asked.

Sally nodded and pulled it out of her pocket. After the events the night before—she didn't want to leave it out of sight. It was comforting to just sit and stare at it. So, she kept it the whole day.

His outstretched hand took a hold of it. Nick wrapped his gloved hands around the globe and vigorously shook it. The snow and glitter fell across the tiny landscape inside again. And like the day Nick gave it to her, it began to snow unannounced.

"Sally, what is God telling you right now?"

"Nothing."

"Take the globe. Shake it. And then tell me what He says."

Nick handed Sally back the little sphere. She shook it and watched the scattering snow and glitter. There was something new inside. A Christmas tree with presents—wait—her Christmas tree. And Sally saw herself sitting next to the tree opening a gift.

Nick smiled.

"How can this be?"

"Look closer."

She found herself sitting on the couch back at the farm. Christian sat on the floor next to the Christmas tree. He was holding a gift.

Sally knelt forward and wrapped her arms around him. "Christian?"

"Hi, Mommy!" He cheerfully said. "I've made you something."

Sally reached out and took the wrapped package from his little hand. "Thank you honey, you're too sweet."

She opened the gift. The bright, silver blue snowflake wrapping paper lay around her legs. Sally peered inside the small package and gasped at the contents.

"Do you like it Mommy?"

Sally pulled out a folded piece of paper and carefully opened it. Again, like before, it was a picture of Sally praying inside a snow globe. She looked at Christian, "I love it."

"Sally, it's time." Nick said, standing at the living room's entrance.

Sally held up the picture. "Nick, what does this mean?" She felt cold air hit her face. We were back. Christian was gone.

"What do you think it means?" Nick said.

"Nick, I... I can't keep doing this. You have to stop doing this." Why was it when Nick touched the globe, something happened.

"Sally?"

It was Reverend Surls.

"What are you doing outside in the cold?" Concern wrote its name on his face.

"I, um... where's Nick?"

"Who's Nick? You're the only one here."

"Sorry, I just... never mind. I just came out here to get some fresh air. I thought you left for home?"

Bruce laughed. "I was, but I felt compelled to come back. So, I turned my car around and drove back."

"What about your family?"

"They know I'm back in Providence. They'll be fine without me. I'll travel back home tomorrow. Come on; let's get you inside to warm up." Bruce said.

Maybe God sent Bruce to talk with me. If Nick could make something feel real, maybe God could send someone for her. It wasn't out of the realm of possibility. "Bruce, do you believe in angels?"

Okay, that was a stupid question. Of course he believed in them. "What do you know about them?" That was a better question.

"Does this have to do with this Nick you were looking for?" Bruce asked.

Either this man was intuitive—or he knew Nick. That was absurd, how could he know Nick? Unless Nick was... "Yes. He gave me this snow globe the other day. He said I would need it." Sally handed Bruce the snow globe. "He was right you know... I did need it."

"What did he say to you tonight?"

"He asked me if I knew what God was saying."

"And... do you?"

It hit Sally like a freight train. She looked into the dark blue eyes of the preacher. "I'm sorry, I have to go."

"Um... Okay?"

"I'm sorry Bruce, there's something I have to know. Something I missed. I don't know, but I have this feeling." Sally buttoned up her jacket and pulled her gloves on. "Tell everyone I had to go home."

Sally's heart raced as she drove. She felt bad by leaving the Reverend like that. He probably wanted to pray with her. That was fine and all... but this... this was so much more. Something happened this last time Nick touched the globe. There was something mystical about Nick, about the globe and about the dreams.

Were they dreams? Were they real? Could Nick be an angel... or something altogether different? Whatever it was she knew God began speaking for the first time in years.

The snow fell in a fury. The click-clack of the wiper blades passed back and forth across the window non-stop the entire journey back to the farm. They were on full speed.

"God if you're real... let this be." Sally prayed.

This was all a guess of course—but one that she'd gladly make again. "God I need you to make this what I think it is."

The dark, gravel road wound its way to the farmhouse. The truck bounced and slipped on the fresh snow. No time to slow down—she had to get back to the farm. The back end of the truck slid to a hard right. The tires bit past snow into asphalt. Sally yanked the wheel in the direction of the slide and corrected the vehicle from careening into the ditch.

"What does this mean?"

The drive felt a heck of a lot longer than normal. She felt ghastly by leaving Zack back at the hospital with Mom and Dad. *This was important*—at least it felt that way.

"God don't let this be my imagination." Sally prayed again.

ZACK SAT NEXT to Christian. He glanced at the wall behind him—it read 12 O'clock AM. George had left as soon as he heard Sally went back home. *What could be so important?*

"Merry Christmas, Christian." Zack laid his head down on his son's pillow. "I remember when you could just fit in the palm of my hand. Your hand was the size of my thumbnail. You were so small. Your Mom and I were so proud the day you came into our lives."

A single tear formed and fell onto the bed. "I love you, Son."

Marilyn walked over and placed her hand on Zack's shoulder.

He reached up and looked into her eyes. "I'm going to miss him, Mom."

Tears stained Marilyn's face. "I know you are. We all are."

THE SNOW-PACKED driveway crunched under the Chevy's tires as Sally stopped in-front of the farmhouse. She pushed the door open. The cold air bit her skin as she bounded up the steps to the porch. Unlocking the door, Sally stepped through.

She heard their Maltese dog barking. "It's okay, Jack—it's just me." She kicked off her shoes and tossed her coat onto the kitchen floor. The dog tried to crawl up Sally's leg. She reached down and patted his tiny head.

"God, let this be." The years of Christmas past flooded her mind with joy. The dog heeled to her left as she walked into the living room.

"What am I doing?" Sally said, and sat on the sofa. The white dancing Christmas tree lights fell across the room. The smell of apples and cinnamon invited her with their aroma. Each present carefully wrapped itself around the base of the tree. A small Nativity scene sat on the piano adjacent to the tree with Mary, Joseph and baby Jesus. Each had a perfect little smile carved on their wooden faces.

Sally watched the tree intently. The glowing lights bathed the room in a golden hue. One gift caught her attention. It looked familiar. In-fact, the whole scene looked familiar. A curious case of déjà vu—but it wasn't that—it was so much more.

She knelt next to the tree and carefully pulled a bright silver blue, snowflake wrapped gift out. Holding onto it, Sally's throat tightened as the little nametag fell open.

To: Mommy

From: Christian

A tear dripped onto the nametag, smudging the writing. Her hand slid under the tapeline, popping the seam. The wrapping paper ripped off with ease and circled her feet.

She peered inside.

ACTIVITY BUZZED around an Emergency Room at a nearby hospital. An ambulance came back from a deadly accident on the main highway. The paramedics pulled a waiting gurney out.

"What do we have?" asked an ER surgeon.

"A male accident victim. We couldn't save him." The paramedic pulled out a small card. "He's an organ donor."

"ZACK, IT LOOKS like you need some rest."

"I'm fine, Mom." Zack said.

"It's nearly one in the morning."

Zack's hand still held Christian's. He felt a slight squeeze. Zack stood up, "Christian?" Again, another slight squeeze.

"Oh my, Christian!" Zack looked over at Marilyn, Bruce and Rose. "He just moved his hand." He laughed. "My boy just moved his hand."

Smiles filled the room.

His joy shattered, as the heart monitor changed tone. The lines across the screen spiked higher and higher. Fear dug its talons into his heart as the monitor raced.

"I need a doctor in here!" Zack yelled down the hall.

He watched the signal spike and fall, spike and fall. A doctor and nurse rushed into the room.

"What's happening to my boy?"

They looked Christian over.

"Doctor?"

"He's going into cardiac arrest."

The beeping monitor changed sounds again and fell into a long drawn out tone.

Christian, flat lined.

ELEVEN

THE SMALL BOX lay open on Sally's lap. What she saw inside shook her to the core. Not expecting to find what she was looking for—yet, there it was in her hand—a carefully folded piece of paper. Sally unfolded it. The stars aligned as the picture fell open in her hands.

Red, gold, brown and purple swirled in the picture. There was no mistaking what she saw. A snow globe. Inside the drawn snow globe, a picture of Sally praying. Christian knew, though she didn't fully understand it—but Christian knew.

The first dream came rushing back. *"Are you praying for me Mommy? I need a new heart."*

Sally had prayed. She prayed God would spare her son. She tried everything to be strong. Yet, Zack was the strong one. And she pushed him away. A wave of raw emotion washed over Sally and she began to sob uncontrollably.

All I've done is cry and be mad at God.

All God did was reach out and say, *"Here I am. I've never left you."*

Sally, for the first time in years, knelt and began to pray. "God, I've not been the strong one. I don't even know what to think, say or do. It's been so hard. My little boy is dying and there's nothing I can do. I need your help. Christian needs a new heart in order to live."

"CLEAR!"

Christian's body jerked as the electrical current passed into his heart.

Nothing.

The paddles charged again, "Clear."

A faint heartbeat slowly showed itself on the heart monitor.

Another nurse came into the room and whispered in the doctor's ear.

Zack watched the event unfold before him. He had to call Sally, but he couldn't tear himself away to make the call.

"Tell them to prep the operating room. We're going in." The doctor said, then pulled up the bed railings.

"What's happening?" Zack asked.

"We received word a new heart is on its way. We have to prep him for surgery." The doctor replied.

Zack collapsed to his knees. "Thank you God!"

"Daddy?" Rose said.

"Yes, Rose?"

"Is Christian going to be okay?"

"He's going to be fine. God is taking good care of him right now."

GEORGE WALKED into the house and the dog greeted him. "Hey buddy, where's Sally?"

He walked through the kitchen into the living room where Sally sat. She was staring at a snow globe. George noticed the torn wrapping paper at Sally's feet.

"Hey, Sally." George said softly.

She looked up. She looked glad to see him. "Hey, Dad."

"You okay? Pastor Bruce said you left in a hurry."

Sally tears from her eyes. "Yeah, I had to come home. Needed to check something." She gazed at the flittering snow, falling on the tiny landscape in the snow globe she held.

"We were worried about you, so I thought I'd come over and see how you're doing."

"Thanks, Dad. I appreciate that." Sally said.

"Sally," George began, "God really does love you. You know that, right?"

"It's so hard right now. Life is hard. I've forgotten how to trust in

God."

"Sally, Mom's favorite Bible verse is in the book of Proverbs. *"Trust in the Lord with all your heart..."* You have so much to live for."

"After the death of Gideon, I stopped trusting in God. Gideon was such a lovely brother... and I pushed him. Dad, he'd be here today if I didn't hadn't push him away."

Compassion filled his heart for his daughter. There were things she needed to deal with past demons that haunted her. And tonight, she was dealing with those demons.

"Sally, you're right, life is hard—but it's what we do with our life that matters."

Sally shifted her weight and showed him the snow globe. "Dad, when Nick gave this to me... it felt as if God was saying—*hey it's okay, you can trust Me.* Nick told me this would bring comfort during a terrible tragedy. In a strange way, Nick saved my life. I was angry and Nick pointed that out by his continual kindness. Dad, tonight was the first time I've began trusting God again. I prayed!"

So, this is what Nick meant by being here for Sally. She needed to begin trusting in God. And George, being her father, knew how to do just that. After Gideon's death, George had to trust in God—it was all that was left for him at that moment.

"Can I pray for you?" George asked.

"I would love that." Sally said.

When George finished praying the phone rang.

DOCTOR DAVIS SHEETS stepped into the operating room. A waiting gown for him was placed on a hook. He scrubbed his hands and allowed someone to dry, dress and put gloves on him.

"Alright folks, are we ready?" Davis quickly glanced the room over; making sure everything was in place. "Okay people, we only have one shot at this, let's make it count."

The new heart had been placed in a stainless steel bowl filled with ice. Christian was prepped before Davis arrived. He grabbed a small, yet sharp, surgical scalpel and proceeded to make an incision over the sternum.

"Okay," Davis left his hands on Christian's chest. "let's open him up."

THE TRIP TO the hospital blurred by. A glimpse of hope filled Sally's heart. God answered her prayer. It was something she thought would never happen. Their family was in the lounge waiting, when George and Sally arrived. An eternity passed since they sat here two days prior. Could it have only been two days since Christian fell through the ice? Now, they sat waiting for the prognosis of his second surgery.

"How long has he been in?" Sally said.

Zack walked over and hugged her. With a light kiss on the cheek he said, "He's been in about thirty minutes. We don't know how long it is going to be."

Sally sat down and exhaled. This was going to be a long night. Zack came over and sat next to her. He had to know. She had to let Zack know she'd forgiven him. Sally placed her left hand on his cheek. "I prayed, Zack. I prayed God would provide a heart for our boy."

He smiled, "I know, so did I."

"Zack..." She felt another sob. "You apologized to me—I got angry. You're my best friend and I don't want anything to come between us. I'm so sorry for the way I treated you... will you ever forgive me?"

Zack leaned forward pulling her lips to his. "Sally... I will always love you. Nothing will ever change that."

She smiled and turned to her parents. "Mom, Dad. I need to ask your forgiveness also."

"What is it dear?" Mom asked.

"When I went home, Dad helped me remember something you taught me. You taught me and Kaitlyn to trust in God, no matter what. Before, during dinner, I left angry and I'm sorry."

"You're forgiven Dear." Dad said.

"I had to get out of this place, so I stepped outside for some fresh air. Nick showed up again. He told me God would never let me go through something I couldn't handle. At first, I didn't know if I could handle it. And then, I found this under the Christmas tree at home."

Sally pulled out the picture, the one Christian drew, and handed it to Zack.

Zack's eyes said it all. "Sally? This looks like the same globe that... how can that be?"

"It is." Sally grabbed Zack by the hand. "And while on the living room floor, I asked God to forgive me—just like you did earlier today with Bruce. The words you spoke to me came back as I sat staring at this picture Christian drew. I knew I had to ask Jesus to forgive me."

Sally, in that moment, knew she was clean. No, *whole*. And looking into her husband's smiling eyes Sally knew she had her husband and her faith back.

CHRISTIAN HAD BEEN in surgery for nearly five hours before the Doctor arrived. "Everything went smoothly. The new heart works just fine—like it's supposed to."

"How long before he can come home?" Sally asked.

"It could be anywhere from a week to two weeks. It all depends on his recovery."

"Thank you for everything, Doctor Sheets." Zack said.

"You're welcome. And Christian was one of the lucky few who get their new heart. It seems as if someone has been watching over Christian this whole time." Doctor Sheets smiled.

Someone had been watching over all of us. "May we go see him?" Sally asked.

"Yes, he just woke up about a half-hour ago. We're still monitoring him—so Zack and Sally, you are allowed in the room. The rest of the family will be able to see him soon."

Christian was going to be okay. It only took a moment before they were standing at the door. Sally felt someone watching her intently. She turned and smiled at Nick.

"I'll be right back, Zack." Sally said, and headed over to the old man.

"Hello, Sally." He said warmly. "Looks like Christian is going to be alright."

"He is." Zack was watching. "Can I ask you something, Nick?"

"Sure."

"Who are you?"

Nick let out a slight laugh, "Sally, you have learned to trust in God with your heart. It took a hardship for you to learn it. The sad thing is, some never learn about the gift of life. Someone had to die in order for Christian to live. And the same is true with you and Zack."

He didn't answer the question. "But who are you?"

Nick smiled and something in his eyes sparkled. "Sally, I think you already know who *I Am*." He took Sally's hands. "You're my child, Sally. I made you special—I needed a good mother to look after Christian. You prayed. And I answered. It's as simple as that."

Nick turned around and walked down the hall. Sally watched him vanish into thin air.

"You coming?" Zack called.

Sally smiled. Her heart was warm and clean. Christian was going to live. And she knew something that changed her life forever. One snowy day, a graying old man gave her a snow globe and that day her life changed.

"Sally?"

"I'm coming." Sally turned and walked into the recovery room with her husband. At that moment, she knew the greatest gift on earth was hers. The gift of life. It was by Divine Providence Nick showed up when he did. Maybe Nick *was* an angel or maybe something more—only God knew.

Sally closed the door behind her and took hold of Christian's hand.